Dear Parents:

Congratulations! Your child is taking the first steps on an exciting journey. The destination? Independent reading!

STEP INTO READING® will help your child get there. The program offers five steps to reading success. Each step includes fun stories and colorful art or photographs. In addition to original fiction and books with favorite characters, there are Step into Reading Non-Fiction Readers, Phonics Readers and Boxed Sets, Sticker Readers, and Comic Readers—a complete literacy program with something to interest every child.

Learning to Read, Step by Step!

Ready to Read   Preschool–Kindergarten
• big type and easy words • rhyme and rhythm • picture clues
For children who know the alphabet and are eager to begin reading.

Reading with Help   Preschool–Grade 1
• basic vocabulary • short sentences • simple stories
For children who recognize familiar words and sound out new words with help.

Reading on Your Own   Grades 1–3
• engaging characters • easy-to-follow plots • popular topics
For children who are ready to read on their own.

Reading Paragraphs   Grades 2–3
• challenging vocabulary • short paragraphs • exciting stories
For newly independent readers who read simple sentences with confidence.

Ready for Chapters   Grades 2–4
• chapters • longer paragraphs • full-color art
For children who want to take the plunge into chapter books but still like colorful pictures.

STEP INTO READING® is designed to give every child a successful reading experience. The grade levels are only guides; children will progress through the steps at their own speed, developing confidence in their reading.

Remember, a lifetime love of reading starts with a single step!

Published in the United States by Random House Children's Books, a division of Penguin Random House LLC, 1745 Broadway, New York, NY 10019, and in Canada by Penguin Random House Canada Limited, Toronto.

Step into Reading, Random House, and the Random House colophon are registered trademarks of Penguin Random House LLC.

Visit us on the Web!
StepIntoReading.com
rhcbooks.com

Educators and librarians, for a variety of teaching tools, visit us at RHTeachersLibrarians.com

ISBN 978-1-9848-4982-3 (trade) — ISBN 978-1-9848-4983-0 (lib. bdg.) —
ISBN 978-1-9848-4984-7 (ebook)

Printed in the United States of America
10 9 8 7 6 5 4 3 2 1

ILLUMINATION PRESENTS

THE SECRET LIFE OF

PeTs 2

I AM
CAPTAIN
SNOWBALL!

by Dennis R. Shealy
illustrated by Michael Borkowski

Random House 🏠 New York

I watch over this city.
I protect its pets
and people.

I do all kinds of other
superhero stuff.
For I am . . .

. . . Captain Snowball!

But I was not
always a hero.

I hated humans
and wanted to
do them harm.

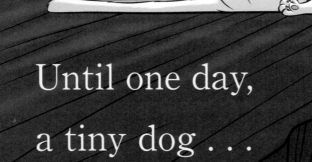

Until one day,
a tiny dog . . .

. . . and a little girl's love
showed me the error
of my ways.

From that day forward,
I vowed to never be
a bad bunny again.

But if YOU are
an evildoer,
then prepare to meet
my furry fists of fury.

I call them
Paw and Order!

When crime calls,
I answer.
And let me tell you,
crime does NOT like
my answer!

I am also pretty sure
that I can fly.

I can do karate

with carrots . . .

. . . and they give me
super eyesight!

Bad guys cannot sneak
up on me. Yikes!

When I am not protecting
the innocent,
I am eating cereal
with my girl, Molly.

We have meetings
and tea parties.

And I let her win
at our favorite
video games.

Because the most important superpower is to be lovable and snuggleable.